Dear Parent:

Congratulations! Your child is taking the first steps on an exciting journey. The destination? Independent reading!

STEP INTO READING® will help your child get there. The program offers books at five levels that accompany children from their first attempts at reading to reading success. Each step includes fun stories, fiction and nonfiction, and colorful art. There are also Step into Reading Sticker Books, Step into Reading Math Readers, and Step into Reading Phonics Readers—a complete literacy program with something to interest every child.

Learning to Read, Step by Step!

Ready to Read Preschool–Kindergarten
• big type and easy words • rhyme and rhythm • picture clues
For children who know the alphabet and are eager to begin reading.

Reading with Help Preschool–Grade 1
• basic vocabulary • short sentences • simple stories
For children who recognize familiar words and sound out new words with help.

Reading on Your Own Grades 1–3
• engaging characters • easy-to-follow plots • popular topics
For children who are ready to read on their own.

Reading Paragraphs Grades 2–3
• challenging vocabulary • short paragraphs • exciting stories
For newly independent readers who read simple sentences with confidence.

Ready for Chapters Grades 2–4
• chapters • longer paragraphs • full-color art
For children who want to take the plunge into chapter books but still like colorful pictures.

STEP INTO READING® is designed to give every child a successful reading experience. The grade levels are only guides. Children can progress through the steps at their own speed, developing confidence in their reading, no matter what their grade.

Remember, a lifetime love of reading starts with a single step!

In memory of Dad, "Duck Taper" of the World
—M.M.

For George
—A.W.

Published in the United States by Random House Children's Books, a division of Random House, Inc., New York, and simultaneously in Canada by Random House of Canada Limited, Toronto.

www.stepintoreading.com

Educators and librarians, for a variety of teaching tools, visit us at
www.randomhouse.com/teachers

Library of Congress Cataloging-in-Publication Data
McDonald, Megan.
Shining Star / by Megan McDonald ; illustrated by Andréa Wallace.
p. cm. — (Step into reading. A step 3 book)
SUMMARY: Star has good times with her friend Blister, but her big sister, Ivy, is still a pain.
ISBN 0-307-26340-1 (trade) — ISBN 0-307-46340-0 (lib. bdg.)
[1. Friendship—Fiction. 2. Sisters—Fiction. 3. Stars—Fiction.] I. Wesson, Andréa, ill. II. Title.
III. Series: Step into reading. Step 3 book.
PZ7.M1487 Sh 2003
[Fic]—dc21 2002015937

Printed in the United States of America First Edition 10 9 8 7 6 5 4 3 2 1

STEP INTO READING® STEP 3

Shining Star

by Megan McDonald
illustrated by Andréa Wallace

Random House New York

DUCK TAPE

One morning, Star was drawing
with chalk on the sidewalk.
Along came Blister on his bike.
Tha-thump. Tha-thump.
"What's that noise?" asked Star.
"It sounds like
a sick washing machine."

“Flat tire,” said Blister.

The tire was squashed.

The tire was smooshed.

“We can fix that,” said Star.

She got her bike pump.
They took turns pumping air
into Blister's tire.
"Good as new," said Blister.

Blister rode down the street and back.

Tha-wump! Tha-wump!

"Sounds like a broken-wing duck
trying to fly," Star said.

"Flat tire again!" said Blister.

“Maybe gum will fix it,” Star said.

“Bubble gum!” said Blister.

Star and Blister stuck gum over the hole in the tire.

Blister rode in circles around
Mrs. Ling's cat, Jasper.

Blister rode in circles around
Mrs. Ling's dog, Coco.

A pebble stuck to the gum.

Ba-loomp. Ba-loomp.

"Sounds like marbles in a tin can," said Blister.

"My sister Ivy has tape that fixes anything."

Star ran into the house.
She came back with a roll
of shiny silver tape.

"Duck tape!" Star said.

"Why is it called duck tape?" asked Blister.

"I guess because it can fix even broken-wing ducks!" said Star.

They pumped up the tire again.
They wrapped it with duck tape.
Once. Twice. Three times.

Blister rode in circles.

Around the chalk drawings.

Around Jasper and Coco.

Up the street and back.

"No more broken-wing ducks!"

said Blister.

"Good as new!" said Star.

They duck-taped Blister's flashlight.

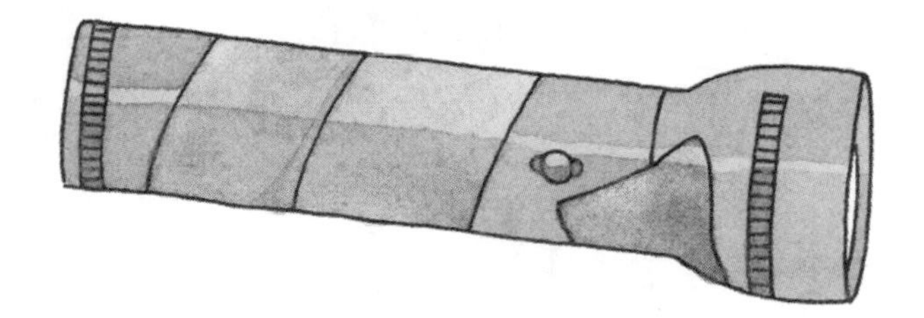

They duck-taped Star's backpack.

They duck-taped Ivy's baseball glove.

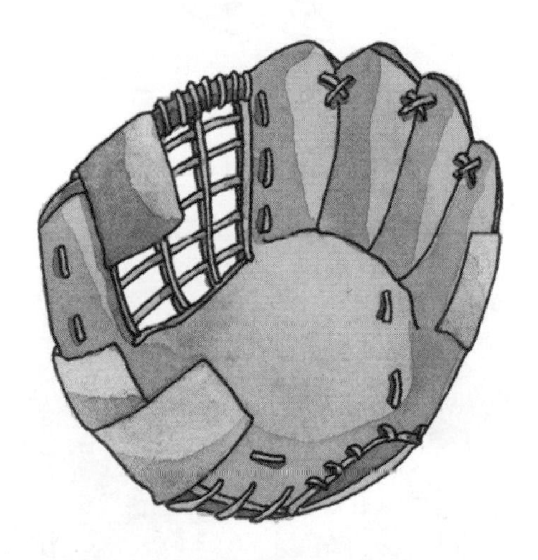

Coco barked.

He grabbed the roll of tape

and ran over to his doghouse.

"Coco! Give it back!" Star said.

Coco barked and barked.

Star and Blister looked at the doghouse.

They looked at the sign that said COCO.

It was falling off.

They duck-taped the sign
on Coco's doghouse.
"Good as new!" said Blister.
"Ivy was right," said Star.
"Duck tape fixes anything!"

Coco licked Star.

Coco licked Blister.

"*Arf!*" said Coco.

STARRY NIGHT

Star ran out of things to duck-tape.

She decided to paint instead.

Blue, blue, blue.

She painted light blue.

She painted bright blue.

She painted dark blue.

STAR

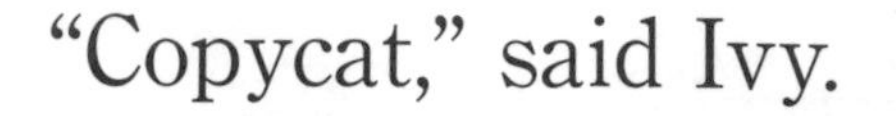

"Copycat," said Ivy.

"Why am I a copycat?" Star asked.

"Picasso," said Ivy.

"Who?" asked Star.

"He is only the king of modern art," said Ivy.

Ivy showed Star her art book.

"He painted pictures all in blue when he was in a bad mood."

"I was not in a bad mood," said Star. "But I am now."

StaR

Star did not want to be a copycat.

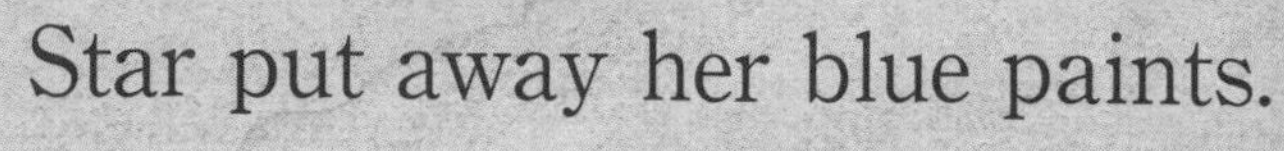

Star put away her blue paints.

Snip, snip, snip!

Star cut happy shapes
out of jelly-bean colors.

Leaves and squiggles and the letter S.
She glued the jelly-bean colors
to the paper.
The shapes danced on the page.
A good-mood painting!

"Copycat," said Ivy.

"Why am I a copycat?" asked Star.

"Matisse."

"Who?" asked Star.

"He is only the king of color," said Ivy.

"He was sick in bed and could not paint.
So he cut out shapes and
glued them to paper."

Stan

Star did not want to be a copycat.
Star took out her markers.
Blue and yellow and red
and green and black.

She wanted to make a painting
all her own.
She made hundreds of tiny dashes
and dabs.
She drew houses and trees out of dashes.
She drew stars and moons out of dabs.

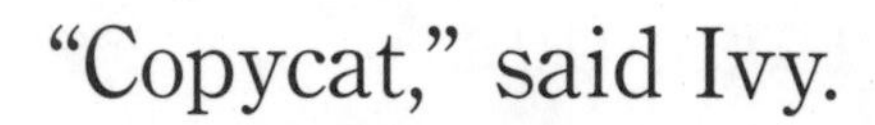
"Copycat," said Ivy.

"Now why am I a copycat?" cried Star.

"Van Gogh," said Ivy.

"Van who?"

Ivy showed Star a painting
full of tiny brushstrokes like dabs.
The painting was called
The Starry Night.
Star did not want to be a copycat.
She did not want her stars to swirl.
She wanted them to shine.
Star had an idea!
An idea all her own.

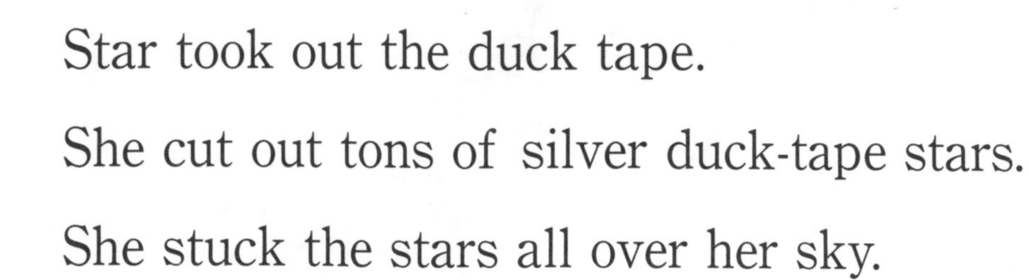

Star took out the duck tape.

She cut out tons of silver duck-tape stars.

She stuck the stars all over her sky.

Her sky was shiny.

Her sky was silver.

Her sky was her own.

“There,” said Star.

“I bet Picasso and Matisse

and Van Gogh

never thought of duck tape!”

SHOOTING STARS

Blister came over for pizza.

"Tonight's the night," Star told Blister.

"Tonight's the night for what?"

asked Blister.

"Star watching!" said Star.

"We might see shooting stars.

They said it on the news."

"Shooting stars!" said Blister.

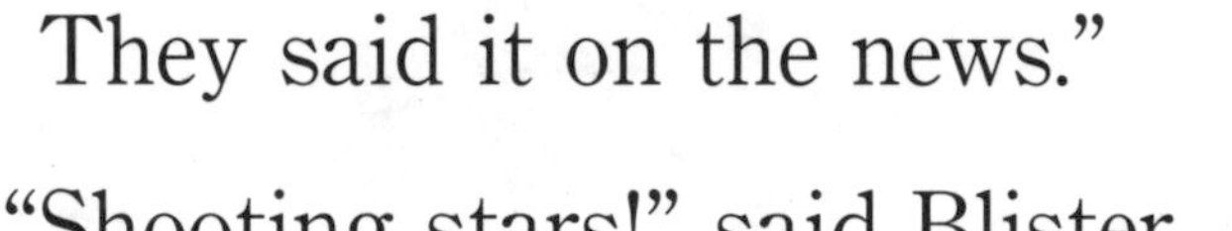

Star and Blister waited past dinner.
Star and Blister waited past sunset.
Star and Blister waited
till it was very, very dark.

Then Star stuffed a blanket and cookies
into her duck-taped backpack.
Blister held the duck-taped flashlight
while Star spread out the blanket
in her backyard.

"Turn off the flashlight," whispered Star.

It was very, very dark.

The sky blinked

with hundreds of tiny dots.

The sky winked with stars.

"It's a starry, starry night!" said Star.

"It looks like your painting

with the duck-tape stars!"

said Blister.

"Thank you," said Star.

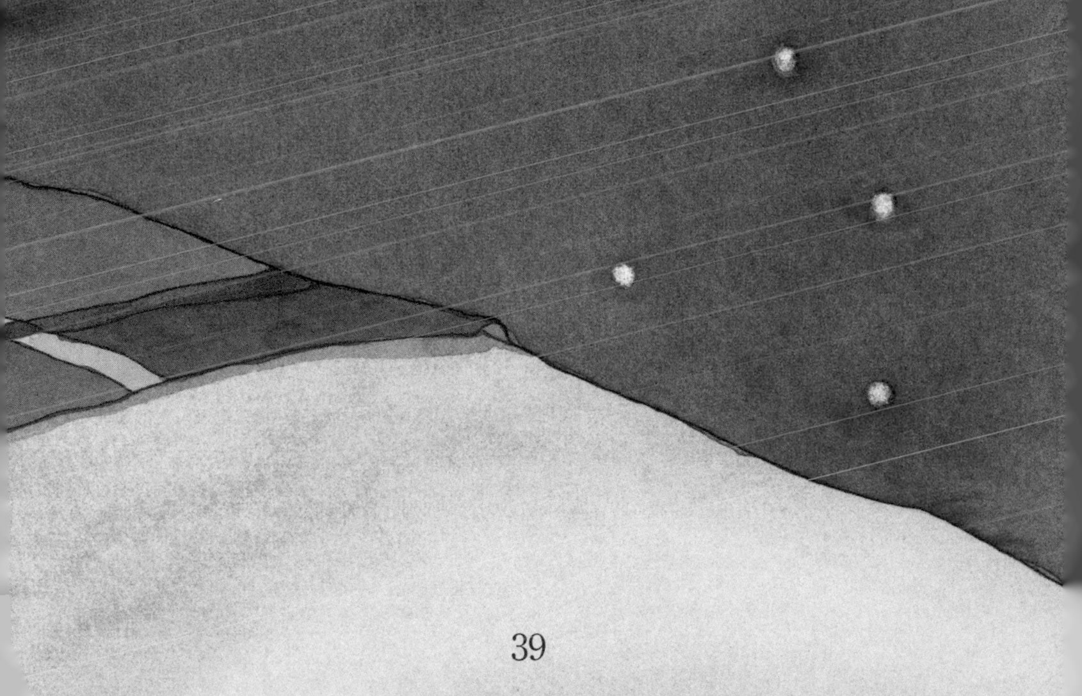

Star and Blister gazed up at the sky
and watched for shooting stars.
Star and Blister ate all the cookies.
They waited and watched
and watched and waited.

"My neck hurts," said Blister.

Star and Blister stretched out on their backs and stared up at the sky some more.

Still they did not see one shooting star.

“The news was wrong,” said Star.

“I guess I’ll go home,” said Blister.

He walked across the street.

Star put on her star pj’s.

Star brushed her teeth

with sparkly toothpaste.

Star looked out the window.

She blinked the light at Blister.

Once. Twice.

Two blinks meant good night.

Star and Blister always blinked lights

before they went to sleep.

Blister blinked back.

Once. Twice.

Just then,
without even looking,
Star saw another light.
Not a Blister light.
A bright light.
A fast light.
A glow-in-the-dark,
streak-through-the-sky light.
A shooting star!

Blister blinked his light at Star.

On-off-on-off-on-off!

Star blinked back at Blister.

On-off-on-off-on-off!

Blister had seen the shooting star!

Star crawled under her quilt,
thinking fall-asleep thoughts.

Blister crawled under his covers,
thinking fall-asleep thoughts, too.

Star and Blister fell sound asleep
under the same shooting-star sky.